A Note to Parents and Caregivers:

Read-it! Readers are for children who are just starting on the amazing road to reading. These beautiful books support both the acquisition of reading skills and the love of books. In some books, there are common sounds at the beginning, the ending, or even in the middle of many familiar words. It is good preparation for reading to help students listen for and repeat these sounds as part of having fun with words.

The RED LEVEL presents familiar topics using common words and repeating sentence patterns.

The BLUE LEVEL presents new ideas using a larger vocabulary and varied sentence structure.

The YELLOW LEVEL presents more challenging ideas, a broad vocabulary, and wide variety in sentence structure.

The GREEN LEVEL presents more complex ideas, an extended vocabulary range, and expanded language structures.

When sharing a book with your child, read in short stretches, pausing often to talk about the pictures. Have your child turn the pages and point to the pictures and familiar words. And be sure to reread favorite stories or parts of stories.

There is no right or wrong way to share books with children. Find time to read with your child, and pass on the legacy of literacy.

Adria F. Klein, Ph.D.
Professor Emeritus
California State University
San Bernardino, California

Managing Editors: Bob Temple, Catherine Neitge
Creative Director: Terri Foley
Editors: Jerry Ruff, Patricia Stockland
Editorial Adviser: Mary Lindeen
Designer: Amy Bailey Muehlenhardt
Storyboard development: Charlene DeLage
Page production: Picture Window Books
The illustrations in this book were prepared digitally.

Picture Window Books
5115 Excelsior Boulevard
Suite 232
Minneapolis, MN 55416
877-845-8392
www.picturewindowbooks.com

Printed in the United States of America.

Library of Congress Cataloging-in-Publication Data
Blackaby, Susan.
A fire drill with Mr. Dill / by Susan Blackaby ; illustrated by Amy Bailey
Muehlenhardt.
p. cm. — (Read-it! readers)
Summary: When Mr. Dill, the fire chief, comes to school to talk about fire
safety, something unexpected happens.
ISBN 1-4048-0584-2 (reinforced library binding)
[1. Fire extinction—Fiction. 2. Fire fighters—Fiction. 3. Schools—Fiction.]
I. Muehlenhardt, Amy Bailey, 1974- ill. II. Title. III. Series.
PZ7.B5318Fi 2004
[E]—dc22   2004004520

A Fire Drill with Mr. Dill

By Susan Blackaby

Illustrated by Amy Bailey Muehlenhardt

Special thanks to our advisers for their expertise:
Adria F. Klein, Ph.D.
Professor Emeritus, California State University
San Bernardino, California

Susan Kesselring, M.A.
Literacy Educator
Rosemount-Apple Valley-Eagan (Minnesota) School District

PICTURE WINDOW BOOKS
Minneapolis, Minnesota

"This is a big day," said Mrs. Shay. "Mr. Dill is here to visit. He is the fire chief."

Mr. Dill
Fire Chief

"Can I wear his hat?" asked Kat.

"Will we see his rig?" asked Vic.

"Will he stay for lunch?"
asked Sunny.

"Yes! Yes! Yes!" said Mrs. Shay.

The kids went outside.

Mr. Dill had his big red rig parked in the lot.

Mr. Dill showed the kids the hook and ladder. He let them sit in the driver's seat.

Mr. Dill ran the siren. The kids plugged their ears.

Kat tried on Mr. Dill's hat.

Jess honked the horn.

Vic asked a million questions.

10

Bob hopped on the bumper.

Sunny had fun with the hose.

Mr. Dill told the kids about his job.

"We have to keep the equipment fixed up. We have to rush off when a call comes in. We cannot help people if we are not set to go."

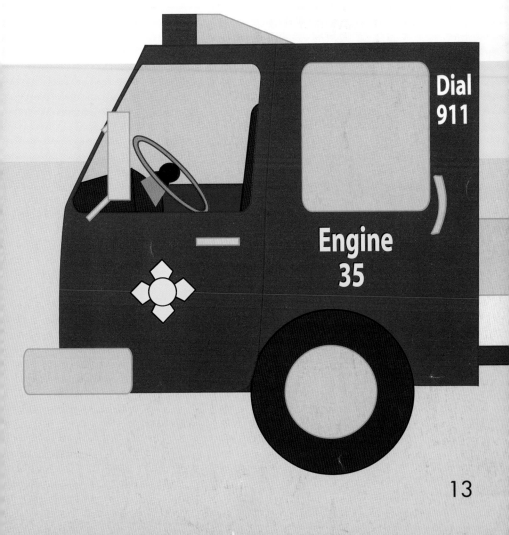

Dial 911

Engine 35

Mr. Dill gave the kids safety tips. "Be sure your house has smoke alarms," said Mr. Dill. "They help keep you safe."

"Be sure you know what to do if
the alarm rings," said Mr. Dill.
"Get down low. Crawl to a door.
Find a way out."

"Then find a grown-up to help you call 9-1-1. We will get to your house lickety-split," said Mr. Dill.

Engin
35

"You can practice at home,"
said Mr. Dill. "Have a family fire
drill. That way you will know just
what to do."

Dial
911

Family Fire Drill

Just then Vic smelled smoke.

He looked at the school.

Smoke billowed out a window.

The kitchen was on fire!

"Quick!" said Vic. "There is a fire! It is in the kitchen!"

The fire alarm buzzed. Kids in other classes marched outside.

"Sit still," said Mr. Dill. Then he ran into the building.

Mr. Dill found Miss Twist in the kitchen. She was throwing black toast into the sink.

"Is there a fire here?" asked
Mr. Dill.

"No," said Miss Twist. "The griddle got too hot. I burned the grilled cheese."

Mr. Dill opened all the windows. He turned on the fan. The smoke cleared.

"This was a close call," said
Mr. Dill.
"You can say that again," said
Miss Twist.

Mr. Dill went back to the kids.

"Miss Twist was in a fix," he said.

"Burning toast makes lots of smoke.
There were no flames. Everything
is OK. Lunch will be a little late."

Dial
911

In a little bit, the kids went for
lunch. Vic sat next to Mr. Dill.

Miss Twist served fish sticks
instead of grilled cheese.
They were delicious.

Levels for *Read-it!* Readers

Read-it! Readers help children practice early reading
skills with brightly illustrated stories.

Red Level: Familiar topics with frequently used words and
repeating patterns.

I Am in Charge of Me by Dana Meachen Rau
Let's Share by Dana Meachen Rau

Blue Level: New ideas with a larger vocabulary and a variety
of language structures.

At the Beach by Patricia M. Stockland
The Playground Snake by Brian Moses
The Word of the Day by Susan Blackaby

Yellow Level: Challenging ideas with an expanded vocabulary
and a wide variety of sentences.

A Fire Drill with Mr. Dill by Susan Blackaby
Hatching Chicks by Susan Blackaby
Marvin, The Blue Pig by Karen Wallace
Moo! by Penny Dolan
Pippin's Big Jump by Hilary Robinson
A Pup Shows Up by Susan Blackaby
The Queen's Dragon by Anne Cassidy
Tired of Waiting by Dana Meachen Rau

Green Level: More complex ideas with an extended vocabulary
range and expanded language structures.

Classroom Cookout by Susan Blackaby
Clever Cat by Karen Wallace
Flora McQuack by Penny Dolan
Izzie's Idea by Jillian Powell
Naughty Nancy by Anne Cassidy
The Roly-Poly Rice Ball by Penny Dolan
Sausages! by Anne Adeney
Sunny Bumps the Drum by Susan Blackaby
The Truth About Hansel and Gretel by Karina Law

A complete list of *Read-it!* Readers is available on our Web site:
www.picturewindowbooks.com